For Trixie.
I can't wait to see what you'll do next.

This book is set in Century 725/Monotype; Grilled Cheese BTN/Fontbros

Printed in Malaysia
Reinforced binding

First Edition, November 2014
10 9
FAC-029191-19042

Visit www.hyperionbooksforchildren.com
and www.pigeonpresents.com

Library of Congress Cataloging-in-Publication Data

Willems, Mo, author, illustrator.
  Waiting is not easy! / by Mo Willems. — First edition.
    pages cm
  "An Elephant & Piggie Book."
  Summary: Piggie tells Gerald she has a surprise for
him, but it is not there yet so Gerald must be patient.
  ISBN 978-1-4231-9957-1
[1. Patience—Fiction. 2. Elephants—Fiction. 3. Pigs—
Fiction. 4. Humorous stories.] I. Title.
  PZ7.W65535Wai 2015
  [E]—dc23   2014007802

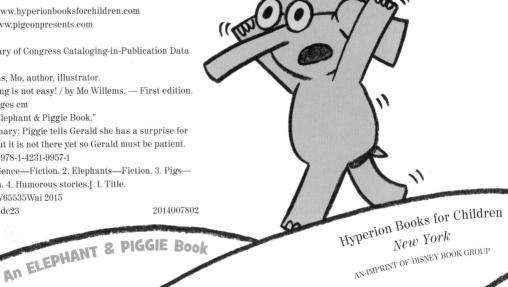

An ELEPHANT & PIGGIE Book

Hyperion Books for Children
New York
AN IMPRINT OF DISNEY BOOK GROUP

Waiting Is Not Easy!

By **Mo Willems**

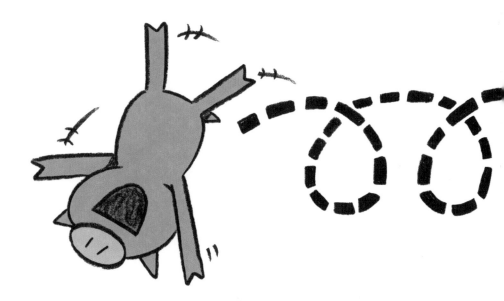

7

11

13

16

The surprise
is not
here yet.

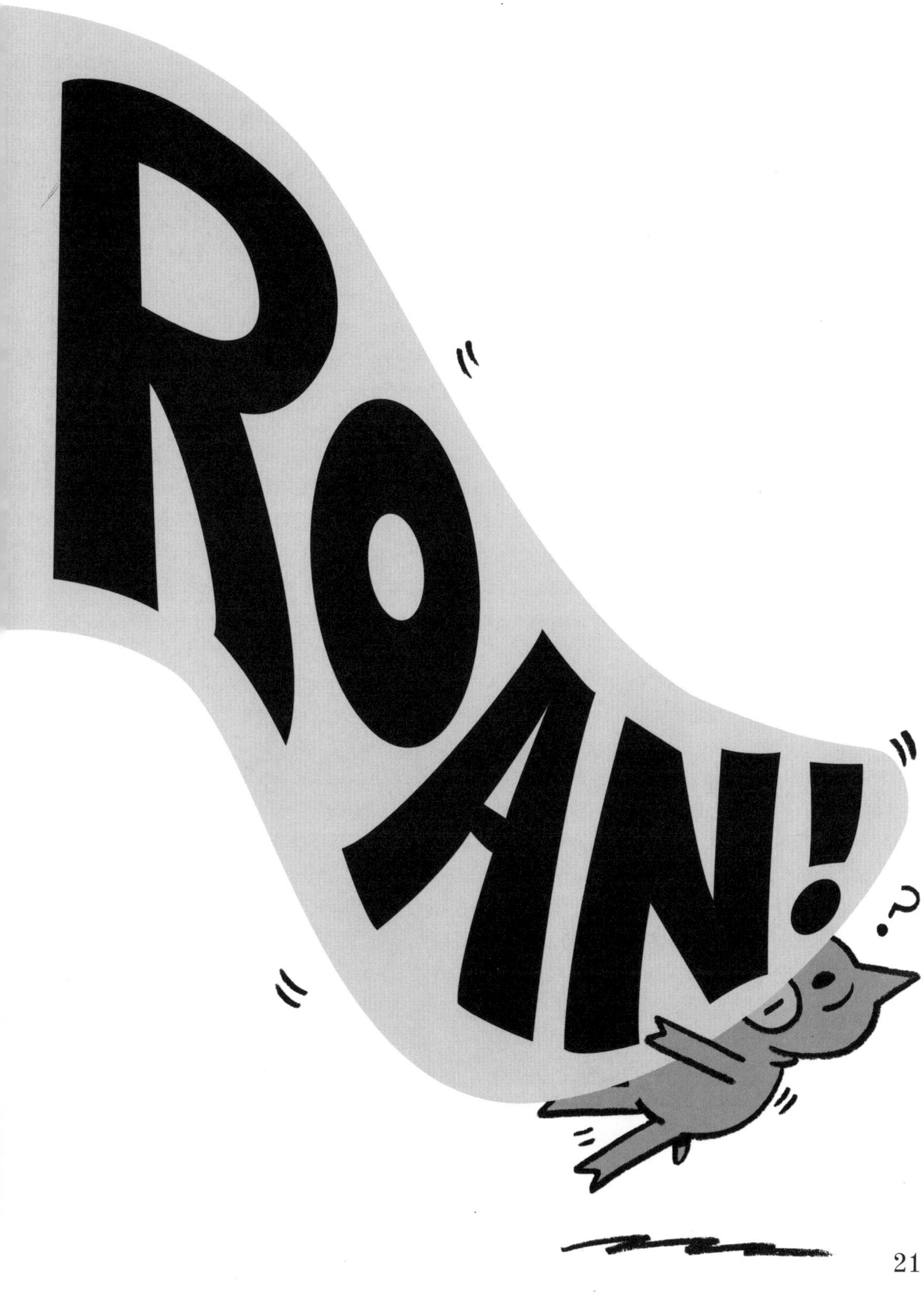
ROAR!
?

Waiting is not easy. . . .

But
we
must
wait.

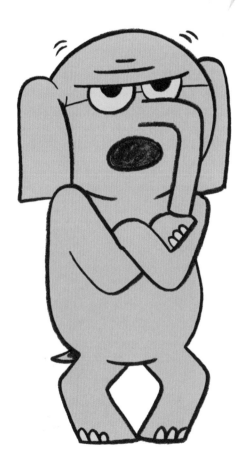

I will not
wait anymore!

Okay. I will wait
some more.

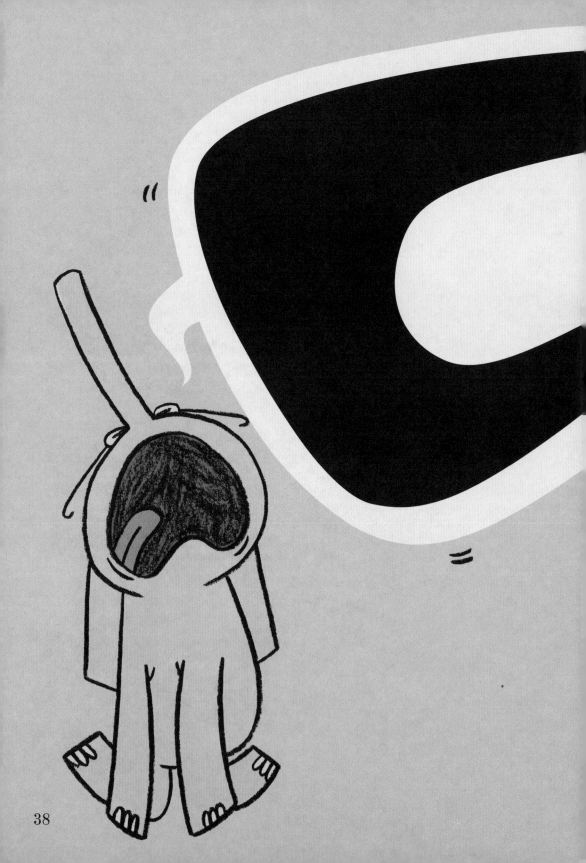

waited and waited and waited!

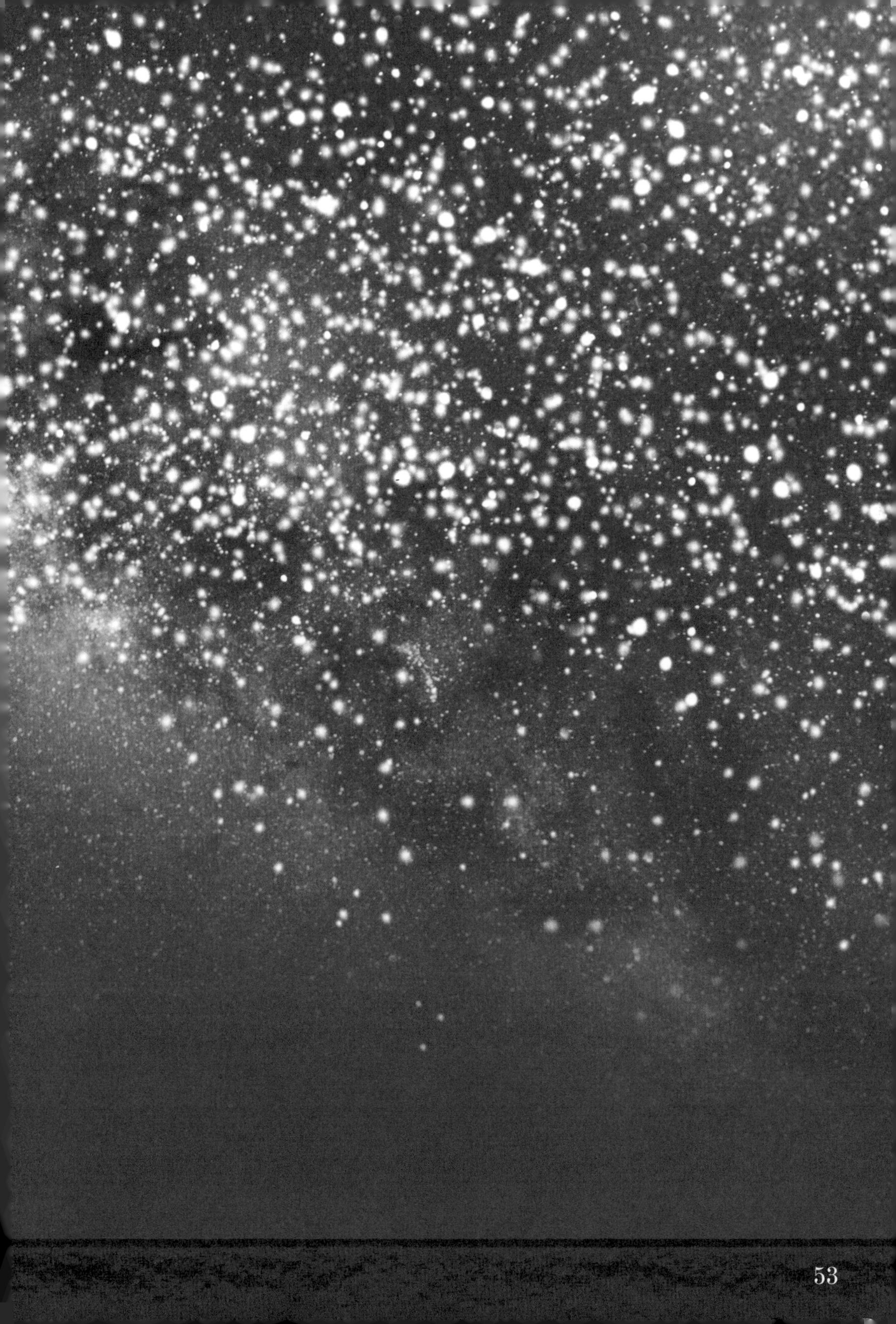

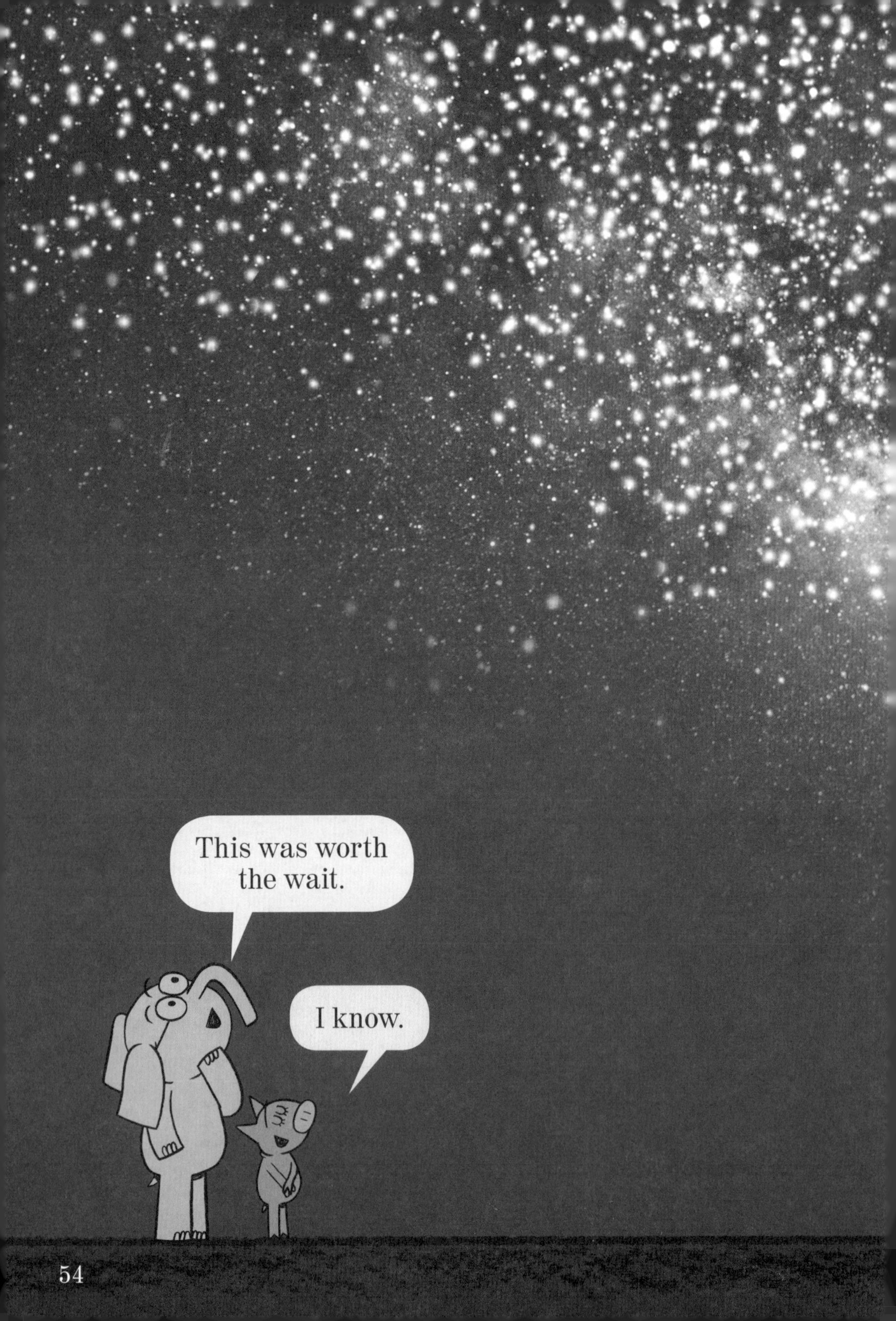
This was worth the wait.
I know.

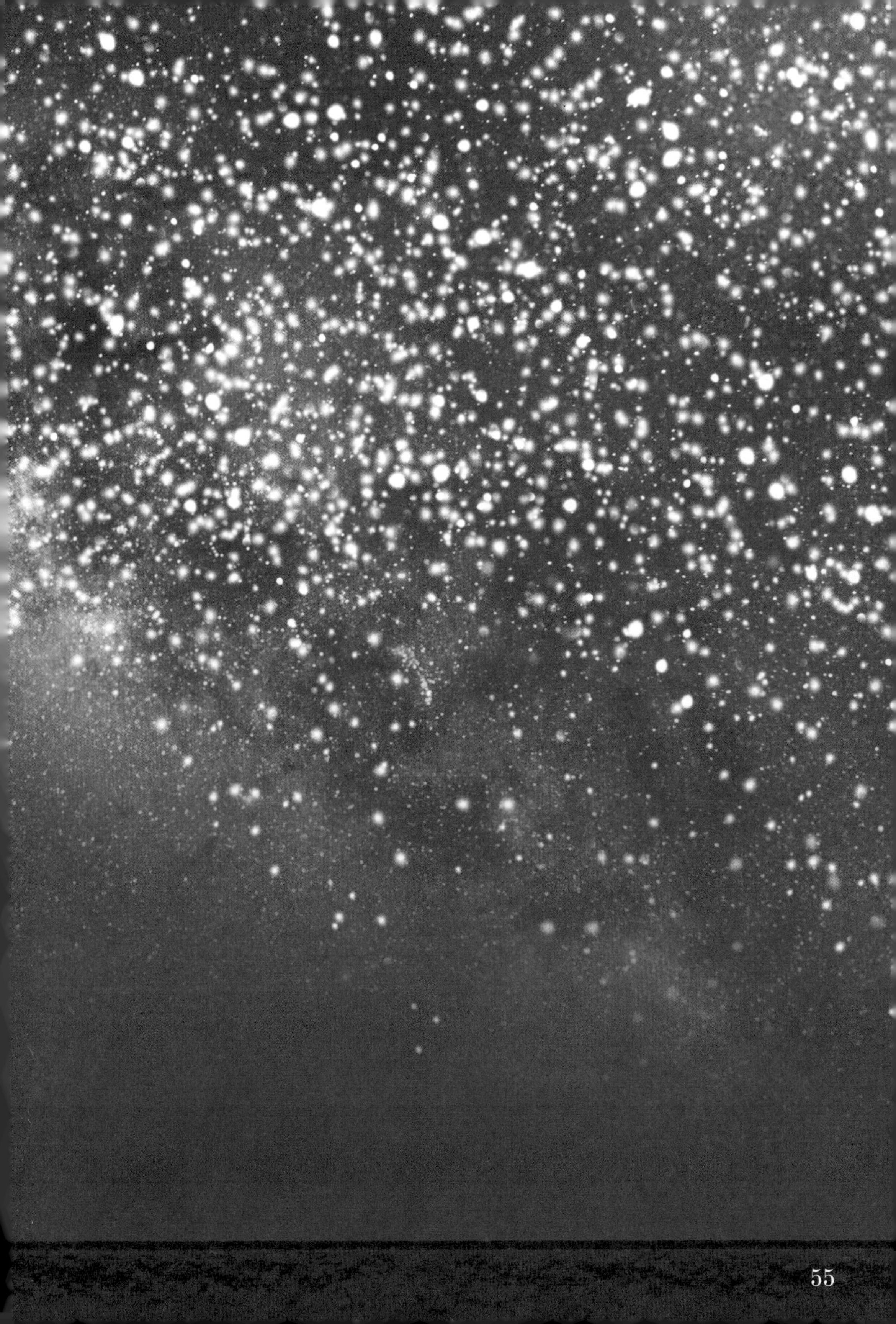

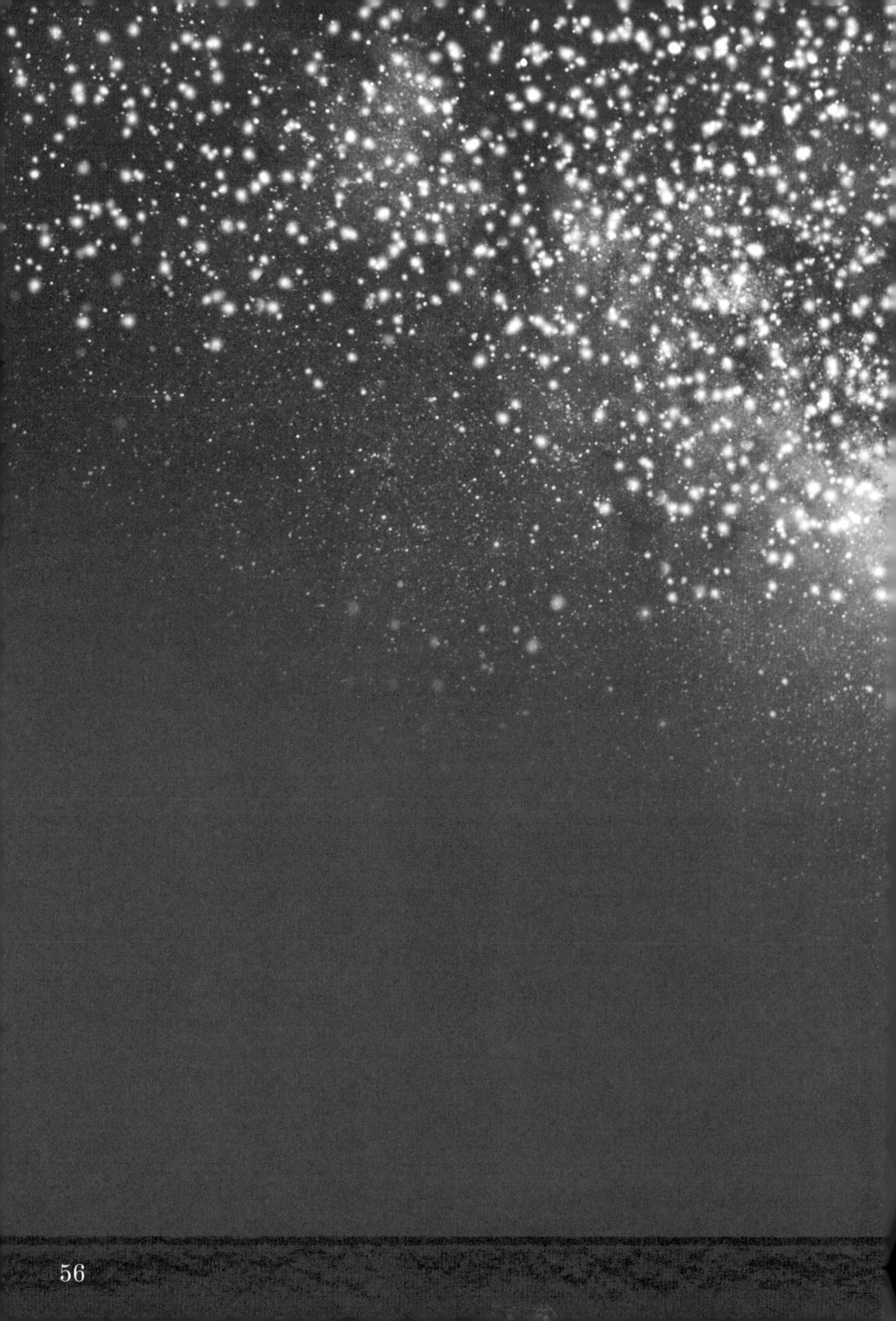

Have you read all of Elephant and Piggie's funny adventures?